Waiting for the Evening Star

ROSEMARY WELLS

paintings by SUSAN JEFFERS

Dial Books for Young Readers *New York*

Special thanks to Caroline, Alexander, and John Cochran;
Catherine VanBrunt; and Baily.

The author and artist wish to acknowledge the generous help
of the staffs of The Billings Farm & Museum in Woodstock, Vermont,
and of Shelburne Museum in Shelburne, Vermont.

Published by Dial Books for Young Readers
A Division of Penguin Books USA Inc.
375 Hudson Street • New York, New York 10014

Library of Congress Cataloging in Publication Data
Wells, Rosemary.
Waiting for the evening star / Rosemary Wells;
paintings by Susan Jeffers.—1st ed.
p. cm.
Summary: Growing up between 1909 and 1917, Berty enjoys
the slow-rolling wheel of time on his Vermont farm
and cannot understand his older brother's desire
to see other parts of the world.
ISBN 0-8037-1398-3.—ISBN 0-8037-1399-1 (lib. bdg.)
[1. Farm life—Fiction. 2. Vermont—Fiction. 3. Brothers—Fiction.
4. World War, 1914–1918—United States—Fiction.]
I. Jeffers, Susan, ill. II. Title.
PZ7.W46843Wai 1993 [E]—dc20 92-30492 CIP AC

The full-color artwork was prepared using watercolor washes over
pencil drawings. Fine-line ink and dyes were then applied.

Under the Elms

On Main Street not so long ago

We knew the songs of different birds,

And how to play a dozen games with words. We knew

Enough was plenty.

And what we didn't know

Could wait till we were twenty.

The elms on Main were cut in 'fifty-five,

But underneath the roots are still alive.

We can say,

"This is now, that was then."

Or take each other's hand and start again.

We had a small farm a mile east of the village of Barstow, Vermont.
The year turned like a wheel. Time went by like a slow song with so many
verses you couldn't count them.

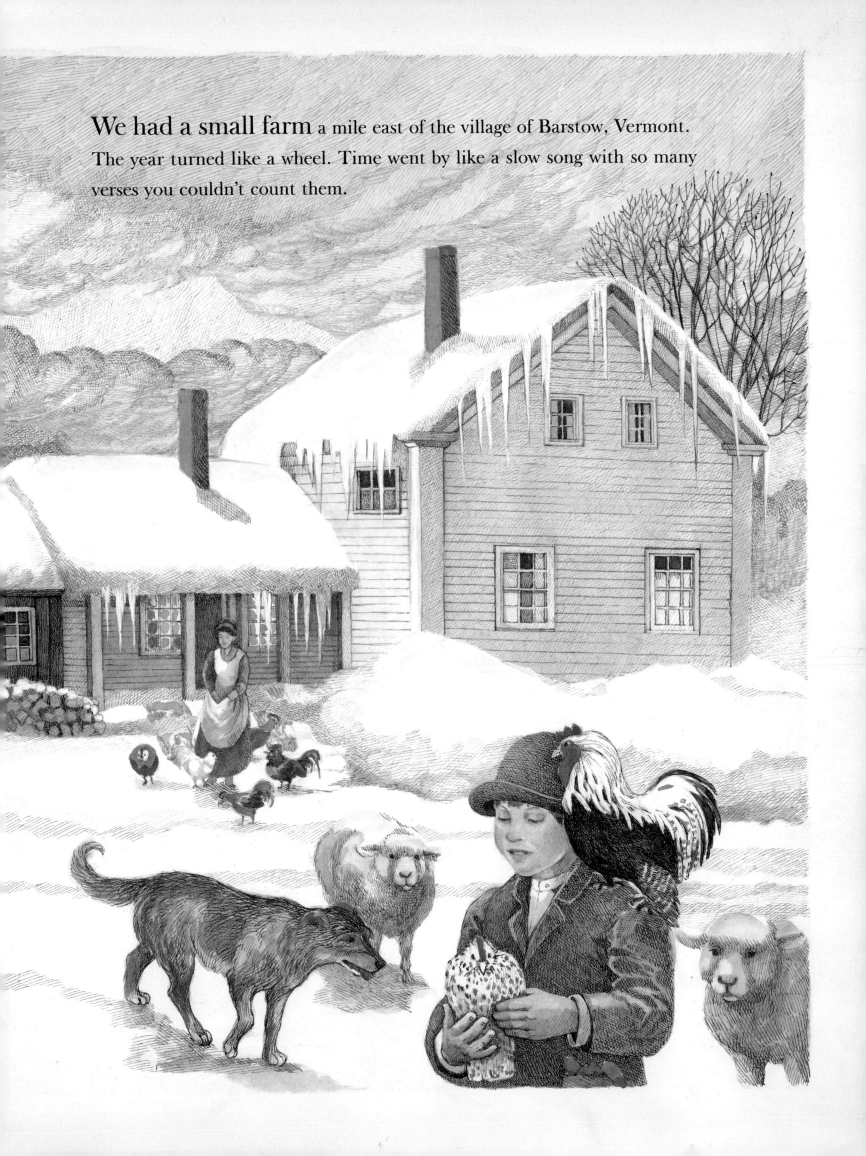

When my brother, Luke, was ten and I, Berty, came up to about Luke's knee, he took me over to Ellis Lake to watch the men cut ice. I was too small a boy to be let stray more than a yard from our fire. But Luke went out to the middle of the lake and held Cal Sewell's two dapple mares, who were hitched to a sled. Luke's hair blew straight away from his head in the early February wind. After our Pa and the other men had swept the lake clean of snow, they marked off a square with a horse pulling an ice plow. When the blocks were cut and the sled was fully loaded, Cal Sewell took the reins from Luke and drove off the lake. George Macready took Cal's place with another sled.

Mama and my grandmother May Bowen brought a barrel of our homemade

cider out to the lakeside. It was heated with cloves and a vanilla bean in it for the men. I helped Grandmother fill the tin cups. She smiled at each man. Their breath came in short clouds of vapor. Their fingers froze in wet deerskin gloves. Each one said, "Thank you, May."

Some of that ice went into our icehouse, which was a deep stone room cut into the north side of our hill. Pa would lop chunks off all summer to keep our milk and eggs cool. Some of the ice was sold hundreds of miles away, down to Carolina. The profit was shared between the cutters and the haulers.

Mama's hot cider was sweet with a little edge on it. It was red as a sunset and made from our own Baldwins and Northern Spies.

When the west wind blew and the snow melted away from the roots of our big elms, sugaring began in Lester Early's woods. Luke and Pa and half the farmers in Barstow went out to tap the trees. Every family brought home enough maple syrup and sugar for the year, plus a profit on every gallon can they produced for Lester Early to sell.

After Sunday dinner in sugaring week Mama poured hot new syrup, clear as a cat's eye, over plates of fresh snow. Luke and I ate it like candy.

The year I was five, Grandmother and I planted the first seeds for our summer garden in pots on the windowsill. The seeds came in the mail in packets with the most beautiful color pictures of the vegetables-to-be.

I said, "Grandmother, I wish all our vegetables would be as big and fat as the ones on the packages."

She said to me, "Berty, keep your eye on that spot in the sky just over the mountains and wait for the evening star. When it comes out, we'll wish on it. Wishes on the evening star are bound to come true."

In six weeks we moved the seedlings to the cold frames on the south side of our house. Sheltered from the wind, they prospered in the daytime sun under the sweating glass. At bedtime, beneath my goose feather quilt, I worried just how warm those pea and carrot sprouts stayed during the cold nights of early spring. But Grandmother was right. Our wish came true. We had carrots as fat as thumbs, and peas enough to feed the birds.

When I was seven, Luke and his best friend, Peter Early, started high school ten miles away in Brandon. In April Luke and I ran into the woods looking for dandelions and fiddleheads. We got baskets of them. We were sick to death of eating winter food—beans and suet pudding. Mama made a salad of the greens with vinegar, sugar, and bacon. This marked the true beginning of spring.

We took what greens we had left over, and a bunch of violets down to Mrs. March. She lived with the Kinney sisters, who had taken her into their big house because she was old and ailing.

On the way home Luke stopped by the railroad tracks, and we watched the Central Vermont 5:19 out of Brattleboro roar by.

"Someday I'll be on that train," said Luke.

We owned three milch cows. Amelia and Big Amelia were Guernseys. The Ayrshire was Red Rita. Mama rose at six, woke the sleepy cows in the barn, cleaned their bags so the milk would not sour, and milked them in about thirty minutes. Late afternoons Luke or I would fetch the cows out of their pasture to be milked again.

Grandmother made cream and butter and cheddar cheese. The cheeses were dyed marigold yellow with carrot water and sealed in great rounds with paraffin. They rested on the shelves of her buttery. When she finished making a tub of butter, she let me stamp the top surface with her own wooden imprint of a thistle flower. A year's worth of table butter bought us a new lamb from our neighbors.

Sometimes she'd give me the first glass of buttermilk left from the catch pan. Even on the hottest days of August her dairy, built on the shady side of the house, was as cool as a May morning.

Pa sold the milk we didn't need to George Macready's creamery at the end of Grant Street. They bought milk from every farm in Barstow and sold butter, cream, and cheese to Boston traders on Saturday mornings.

We were paid on market day. By the time Luke was fifteen, he could drive the wagon to market. When the milk train pulled away, headed for Boston, carrying the gifts of the Amelias and Red Rita, Luke jingled the money we had made in his pocket. He said, "Someday I'll be on a train to Boston. From there I could get on a ship."

Luke wouldn't talk to Pa about this. Pa said the rest of the world was just full of war and foreign languages.

Luke and Pa, Nutt Kaiser, Will Cox, and Peter Early all went out haying together in June. I helped them pitch the fresh-cut timothy grass from the wagon into the loft of our barn before I jumped into it. When the work was done, Pa lifted me out of the loft by the arms. I was as full of hay as a scarecrow. He said, "God's heaven must smell like June hay."

The summer he was sixteen and I was nine, Luke woke one night in the bed next to me. I woke also. "What's the matter, Luke?" I asked, but he wouldn't tell me. Instead he took me out in the hayfield near the tracks and we sat among the fireflies, listening for the train from New York. Like a great beast it hurtled out of the valley en route to mysterious points north.

"Why do you want to leave, Luke?" I asked.

"I want to see what's over the mountains, Berty," said Luke.

Many nights Luke and I tried to see into the train's lighted windows as they flashed by, fast as a comet. Once in a while if the engine slowed, I could look right into a moment of a stranger's life as it slipped past mine. Luke and I dreamed worlds of magic inside those cars, in our own two different ways. Often I fell asleep in a fallen haycock and Luke carried me up the hill home.

On the Fourth of July in the year 1917, Luke was to play first trumpet for the Barstow village band. That year, far away from Vermont, there was a war on. The war had winked at us from distant France like a tiny moon till Peter Early joined the Army. Pete had sent home a photograph of himself in a uniform, smiling in a smooth way I never once saw him smile at home.

Luke practiced his piece, "Columbia, Gem of the Ocean," in the parlor with Mama accompanying him on the piano. Late one night when everyone was asleep, I heard Mama singing a lullaby to herself,

"Sweet and low, sweet and low, Wind of the western sea…
Over the rolling waters go…Blow him again to me."

At the town picnic, I ate a dozen fried oysters, five chicken sandwiches, and two dozen steamer clams; got very sick; and then played baseball all afternoon. Luke, tall and eighteen, was at third base. I backed up the right fielder.

On the walk back home from the picnic that evening, Luke told me he had joined the Navy and would sail to France in two months' time.

"Why, Luke?" I asked.

"The war will be over soon, Berty," he said. "Then I'll have a chance to see the world. Starting with France. Who knows where I'll end up."

"When will you be coming back?" I asked.

"It's a long, costly trip across the ocean, Berty," said Luke.

The walk from Barstow back to our farm that evening was colder to me than an hour in February.

In my pocket was a crumbled chicken sandwich. On the bridge over the river I threw it to the ducks who paddled in the shallows. Cal Sewell had raised the chickens. My mama had made the mayonnaise. My father had cooked the chicken over a grill. Mrs. Early had baked the bread for my sandwich, and I had plenty enough left to feed ducks.

"We have all we need here in Vermont, Luke," I told him. But Luke wanted to be on his way.

August was the longest season in our slow rolling wheel of time. Our fruit trees and garden ripened. For one jubilant month we ate tomatoes, squash, corn, Queen Anne plums, white peaches, and wild huckleberries for breakfast, dinner, and supper.

"In the south of France they have palm trees, and oranges all winter long," said Luke.

"To everything there is a season," said Grandmother.

Near the end of that August, second haying began. I was eleven and big enough to handle a pitchfork in the fields for the first time.

All the men knew Luke was going off to war, and they talked to him in a new way. It was as if he'd been to France already and they were a little shy of him. Pa watched my brother work when Luke's back was turned. Pa grinned and spat on the ground in front of the other men to show how proud he was of Luke without actually saying so.

One day Luke, Pa, the other men, and I had come in about four o'clock. We were grimy with chaff and still running sweat through our shirts. Our hands were rough with callouses and splinters. Grandmother gave Luke a big glass of buttermilk she had cooled for him. He thanked her in words and with his eyes. "I'm going in swimming at Cox's pond," he said.

I watched my brother disappear into the goldenrod, down the sloping meadow. I wanted to shout "Oh, come back, Luke!" but the words stayed shut up tight and hot in my mouth. My grandmother May Bowen turned quickly away from the afternoon light as if it hurt her eyes. I looked up at her, frightened. "What is it, Grandmother?" I asked.

She blinked and smiled at me. Her apron and the hands that held me smelled of warm grass and cream. "Nothing much, Berty," she whispered. "It was only the passing of a shadow over me."

"Mr. Sewell says the war will be over before Luke gets to it, Grandmother," I said, but I was afraid to look into her face.

Luke boarded the southbound train just before sundown, on September 3, 1917. Mama and Pa, Grandmother and I drove him and two suitcases to the railroad depot. Luke waved until I thought his arm would drop off. His hair blew straight out as the train gathered speed.

A sudden truth flooded my heart, although I had no words to put on it then. I was seeing time itself, not the southbound train, carry Luke away. It was time itself I saw uncoil and become an arrow instead of a wheel, heading ever onward to France, land of palm trees, never to return the same.

Luke's vanishing train left an empty sleeve in the air above the tracks. Grandmother took my hand in both of hers and fastened her eyes on the sky just above the hills. "You wait for that evening star now, Berty," she said.

I told the evening star to never let Luke send home a picture of himself in a strange uniform smiling a smooth smile. Then I looked over and watched Grandmother's lips rush through the words of a wish, and the wish itself hurry down the tracks and catch up with the train.